Kreative Futures Ltd

Learning through stories

Leysa

K Cattan

First published in Great Britain in 2017
by Kreative Futures Ltd, Maidenhead, England

Text copyright ©2017 Leysa Henderson
Cover Illustration © 2017 Leysa Henderson – Jack Baker
Designs have the right of use as stated in the contract
Inside illustrations © 2017 Leysa Henderson & Kirsty A Cattan

The moral rights of the author and illustrator have been asserted.

ISBN 978-1-9997833-0-3

Facebook page Eco Children's Books
Twitter follow Kreative Futures
www.kreativefutures.co.uk

Printed and bound in Great Britain by Clays Ltd, St-Ives plc

Dedication

I dedicate this book to my father Brian Henderson who believed in me and just wanted my happiness.

Acknowledgements

Without the love and support of my partner Darren Oakes, I would never have been able to publish this book. Also a huge thank you to Kirsty A Cattan for some incredible illustrations and Sonia Bowker and Alice Fernall for taking the time to read and comment on the story. You have all made it possible.

Foreword

Our planet is slowly being destroyed and every habitable part is being poached by the human race. I couldn't stand by any longer and watch this process continue without taking action. We all have a part to play and a legacy to leave, what that is, is up to each one of us. Once I had made the decision to write about environmental issues through stories, I made space in my life to fulfil that promise.

Orang-utans are losing their habitat at a frightening pace and all for the consumption of palm oil. It was scary to discover how many products use it (over 50%) and how many companies are unaware of the damage and destruction it causes. Rainforests are being destroyed to plant larger and larger areas with palm oil trees. Indonesia intentionally burns thousands of acres each year to clear land quickly and plant vast plantations. It is our job as a consumer to demand that manufacturers source sustainable ingredients, arresting further rainforest devastation. If we don't, then there will be very little wildlife left for future generations to marvel and experience. Once gone, it can never be regained.

Many of the stories about the orang-utans contained within this book are accurate and are multiple. Not just one orang-utan mother is killed and her baby stolen, but many hundreds each year. They are poached, killed and sold to the illegal pet industry all for money. Soon orang-utans will not exist in the wild but will be forced to rely on charities for their survival. This is not acceptable, especially as we could make change now to protect these incredible creatures.

It isn't just the orang-utan that is effected by this land loss, so too are the sun bears, pygmy elephants and rhinoceros as well as many thousands of other creatures and plants. Join with me to make changes so we leave just footprints not carnage behind us.

A percentage of the book's sales will go to protecting the rainforest and their inhabitants; the more books I sell, the greater the percentage of the profits will be donated to wildlife charities around the world. The rest will be used to publish my next book – 'The Woodland King'. Again, a percentage of the profits from that book will be donated to protect British woodlands and wildlife, the rest will go to publishing the next book. This format will continue until I run out of stories.

There is a Facebook page you can follow and add to called Eco Children's Books. Here you will find other book titles that will help to educate your child or yourself on environmental issues. Please feel free to contact me with any book suggestions or interesting videos or pictures which could be shared.

*

We cannot work alone to make change, we need to work as a community. Please join the community and leave our planet a better place than how we found it.

If you are a teacher then you can visit https://www.tes.com/teaching-resource/six-free-planned-units-of-work-to-accompany-the-book-lost-lives-three-chapters-of-the-book-11674317 for free planned resources to accompany the book. Also go to https://www.facebook.com/kreativefuturesltd/ and follow to find out about more resources and other Eco Children books.

Chapter 1

The Book

Walking the streets of this unfamiliar city, Megan knew that her life had to start again. New friends, new school and just another round of bullying. She wondered how long it would take before it would start up again. In her last school, they scarcely gave her time to prove herself. Not that she wanted to, but it felt unfair that no one gave her space or time to be herself; this included her parents. They barely had time for her; she was just a nuisance, someone who created babysitting dilemmas when they wanted to socialise with their so-called friends.

Megan's mother, a fashion victim, could never understand why Megan wanted to dress in oversized T-shirts, striped baseball shoes and baggy trousers held up by a frayed belt, which, by her own admission, would not have looked out of place in the social gatherings of the homeless people of the city slums. For Megan, it was a protest at everything she detested in her own parent's lives. Everything was for show either for the neighbour's sake or the relatives to envy or, even worse, impress the boss.

It was her mum's thirst for perfectionism that created tension within the house and that drove Megan out to seek solace and space from her world. The furniture was being delivered in the morning and her mother was making sure the deliverymen were not going to have a good one.

Snatching up her piccolo and with a heavy heart, Megan slipped out of the backdoor and left the world of chaos behind her.

Megan's inquisitive nature led her to enjoy hours exploring her new city. Roaming the streets allowed her to occupy her mind and escape the rejection and turmoil she felt around her own home and at school.

It was whilst she was immersed in these thoughts that she realised she hadn't been aware of how she'd arrived at this very unusual section of the city. There were narrow, cobbled streets with old signs hanging from shops like flags declaring the end of war or the beginning of peace. Laced between these signs was the washing of those who lived in the upper floor flats above the shops.

Something felt strange, nothing seemed to make sense; it was as if she had stepped into a parallel world. Megan realised that none of the shops' names were familiar; in fact, what they were selling had never featured in Megan's life. One shop, called Sinfin Slattocks Travel Agents, advertised weekend breaks to the age of Arthurian legends; Rotten Rivel, another one, announced the arrival of the slimy alien-like fungi that smelled of rotting corpses and should be fed on rats. In that same shop window, bubbles containing the transparent image of deep sea creatures danced between the jars of floating eyes, snake-like creatures and other weird animals.

Next to that was a sweet shop, which stood tall and proud, only just wider than the stretch of a child's arm length. Its crooked exterior reminded Megan of her history lessons on the Tudor period: black beamed frame with white limed walls. Over time the building had rotated like a twisted spine and then stooped like an old man hunched over a walking stick. The miniature marbled glass door offered a gateway into untold treasures. Multicoloured sweets, piled up meticulously into pyramids, hiding a secret that was only revealed once eaten. Not even the sweet shop owner knew the full effect, as each sweet reacted differently to different people. But what was really strange, was the money. Everything was sold in groats.

'Groats!' exclaimed Megan. 'What on earth are groats?'

People walking passed looked quizzically at her. Suddenly, Megan felt very conscious of her attire. They were all dressed in black robes adorned with a grey sash and a floppy white cap. Colour seemed to have been banished, except in the shop windows.

In amongst these curious shops was one which seemed to call to Megan. From the upstairs window, someone or something was watching her. She thought she saw a face with darkened eyes that penetrated her soul as if they were reading her inner most secrets. Very briefly she caught sight of a ginger rim of light surrounding the face but as soon as she spied the face, it melted into the background. Despite feeling apprehensive and nervous, Megan was drawn to it. Her unconscious mind led Megan to the crooked door.

Carefully, she opened the door and hesitantly stepped inside. What confronted Megan was not what she was expecting. The bookshelves reached up so high that it was impossible to see where they ended. Their height didn't tally with the outside of the shop. Stacks of books were littered all over the floor; they were covered in dust and cobwebs, making it difficult to navigate around the shelves safely.

'It's obvious that no customer has been here for a long time,' muttered Megan under her breath.

Megan loved books, she loved all different types of books as the knowledge they gave empowered her to fight the world from the inside. They gave her experiences and reasoning, which was absent from her own life. Story books would allow her to become another person and enjoy the characters' experiences, their tragedies and finally the happy-ever-after life. Unfortunately, in her life, there was no happy ever after; it was one unhappy experience after another.

Attempting to step over an excessively large pile of books, Megan tripped and fell awkwardly, landing gracelessly on the flagged stone floor. It was then that she noticed she was not alone; out of the corner of her eye she saw a movement emerging from the walls. The temperature dropped dramatically, causing Megan to shiver. Crossing between the shelves, she saw the outline of a figure hobbling towards her. Every nerve cell in her body was alert, fear streamed through her veins leaving her unable to move. She tried to see who was there, or even what was there, but couldn't focus. As suddenly as the shape had appeared, it vanished, but where? She sat trying to quieten her breath and stop the throbbing in her head. This silence allowed her to listen intently for any sound but none could be heard.

Shaking her head and reprimanding herself for her cowardice, Megan stood up and restacked the books as best she could. It was then that she spied the antiquated book lying open. It must have fallen after Megan had knocked the pile over. Squatting down, she wondered what the pictures on the page represented; it was nothing she had ever seen before. Closely scanning the open page, a movement on the map caught her attention. Something had made a splash. Reaching out for the spot, Megan's hand touched water, which made her jump back. Reminding herself that she was not a coward, despite the school playground taunts, she leant forward and touched the spot again, this time her hand met paper and not water. With closer examination, she started to realise that the book was some kind of map. There were hundreds of islands crammed full with Latin names followed by unrecognisable symbols.

Now Megan wished she had not dismissed Latin as a dead language, refusing to attend the classes.

'Is there something you were looking for?' The icy voice cut through the silence, startling her. There was nothing in the voice to indicate that the owner wished to help.

Looking up, Megan found herself staring into the dark, narrow eyes of an old man who showed no pleasure at her presence in his shop. His thin lips were tightly closed in disapproval.

'Nnnno,' she stammered.

'Then I suggest you leave or you find another book to read,' he retorted acerbically.

He glanced briefly at the page Megan had been looking at and then calmly and coldly stared at her making her feel very uncomfortable. She wanted to ask so many questions but realised this was neither the time, nor the place, nor the person to ask.

Megan was reluctant to leave because she wanted to know more about the book of islands. Backing away, she picked up the nearest book and took it to the far corner. She remained in eyesight of the bookseller, watching as he secretly hid the island book behind a wooden panel under the counter. Confident that his hiding place was safe, the bookseller returned to the back of the shop.

Megan's burning curiosity got the better of her. Pretending to leave the shop, she made a lot of noise opening and shutting the door shouting back sarcastically 'Thanks for all your help!' and under her breath, 'And for making me feel very unwelcome.'

Quickly, she hid behind one of the shelves just in time to see the bookseller shuffle to the front of the bookshop and scan the streets. Locking the door and changing the sign to inform his customers that the bookshop was now closed, the bookseller disappeared to the back room to resume his work.

Megan waited to be sure that she was now on her own. Using the faint light that streamed through the dusty windows, Megan found her way to the counter and felt around for the panel. Sliding back the door, she fumbled for the book which again fell open at the same page. Before she had time to even realise what was happening, Megan felt something hit the back of her head hard. There was the sensation of falling into a black hole. Her world was spinning round; pictures of animals, symbols and Latin words whirled behind her eyes and then the hard landing, or at least that was what it felt like.

The last thing she remembered before everything went black was the smell of damp earth.

Chapter 2

A Whole New World

Slowly, Megan began to gain consciousness. Her head ached and the heat was intense. Every now and then she felt something sharp in her back but her body ached too much to turn and see what was stabbing her. There was a strong sense that she was being watched but the fuzziness in her head was just too overpowering so Megan just shut her eyes to block out the pain and confusion.

Eventually, Megan opened her eyes and peered through her heavy eyelids to see the sun shining through the trees. The trees stood straight and high, linked together by vines clinging like a spider's web. There seemed to be no obvious point where one tree stopped and the other started. Abnormally huge leaves leant over Megan and offered some shade against the piercing sun.

The noise around her was deafening, coming from somewhere in the forest was the penetrating sound of an alarm, or that was what it sounded like. Behind her, she could hear fast moving water.

'Where am I?' Megan asked more to herself than anyone else.

Sitting up, she stared in disbelief at her surroundings. Gone was the musty bookshop and in its place was, well, all she could come up with was a rainforest. Megan wasn't exactly sure of this fact as she had never visited one before, but from the books she had read this is how she imagined it to be.

Becoming more alert, Megan realised that she was being watched. It was an intense stare. Looking hard into the green mass she could just make out two dark heavily lidded eyes surrounded by a halo of ginger hair. Then suddenly, it disappeared in a flourish into the depths of the rainforest. It was

definitely not human yet it had the intelligence and intensity of one.

It was then that she heard the shouts and screams of children's voices behind her. Jumping up, she sought refuge behind the large leafed plant and spied two children playing in the chocolate brown river. Creeping slowly towards the riverbank, Megan noticed the dark skin and tight black curly hair, the long thin arms and their wide smiles.

Suddenly, the ground gave way and she found herself sliding, not for the first time that day, towards the chocolate river, stopping just on the bank's verge. Attempting to stand up, Megan realised that her leg was trapped in a tree root; looking up she caught the children's eyes. Their smiles had vanished and were now replaced with fear mixed with confusion. This confusion turned to anger as they slowly moved closer to her. She tried to speak but no sound came out. It was then she felt her loneliness. No one in the world knew or cared where she was. Questions flashed through her mind, how come my life has become so lonely? Was I really such a bad person?

All of a sudden, she felt overwhelmingly resigned to her situation and just smiled. This action took the children by surprise. The older looking child reached out a hand and skilfully released Megan's foot from the twisted root; this resulted in her tumbling into the river. A grubby hand was offered to Megan unsmilingly and, without a word, helped her to her feet. Standing knee deep in dirty brown water, confronted with two staring faces, Megan started to laugh and laugh until her sides ached. The laughter was met with wide-eyed faces and then to Megan's delight they too started to laugh uncontrollably.

She clambered out of the river and all three children lay on the ground until their laughter eventually ceased. When Megan looked closer at the children, she saw their potbellies but, more remarkable was their wide feet covered in thick skin to protect them from the tough thorns and deadly biting insects that lay in wait for unsuspecting victims. The children, noticing her looking at their feet, looked at hers protected by her multicoloured baseball boots. Their faces wrinkled in confusion trying to understand why her feet were covered.

Easily bored with the shoes, they jumped up grabbing her hand and pulled her down to the river where they all clambered into the dug-out and pushed it away from the bank. Floating gently to the centre of the river, they leapt in and disappeared under the water. Both heads popped up and looked at Megan in surprise that she hadn't followed them in.

'Come on, jump in!' the children shouted.

'But what about crocodiles and piranhas?'

'They only come here on Wednesdays, today is Friday, you're OK,' the children laughed.

'But…'

'Jump or we will turn the boat over.'

With one big leap she fell clumsily into the water, scrambled to the surface and saw the laughing faces of her two new companions.

'Come on, lift the boat up and turn it over so we can hide underneath it.'

They all rocked the boat until it turned upside down and ducked underneath. They felt invisible to the world whilst moving slowly downstream.

From far away they heard a deep loud horn. Panic flickered across the two new faces. They turned for the shore and practically ran back. Dragging themselves from under the boat, they grabbed Megan's hand and ran in the opposite direction to the sound of the horn.

They finally reached a small cave alongside the river and gestured for Megan to go in.

'Why have you brought me here?' Megan was feeling a little concerned.

'Ssshhh!' the oldest one said.

He turned to leave her.

'But what's your name?' Megan asked.

'I am Hintu and this is my younger sister Cayru. And yours?'

'Megan.'

With that they ran, disappearing like the eyes she had seen earlier, into the blanket of greenery.

What now? thought Megan grumpily.

Looking around, she found a wide flat stone to perch on. The time ticked by allowing her to think about her situation and wonder how she'd got there.

It must have been that book or was it the bookseller? Megan tried to order her thoughts. There was the thud on the back of the head that could only have come from the bookseller. He must have seen her and crept up behind her. But then how did I get here? She thought. Maybe this was how the bookseller disposed of the bodies.

Her thoughts began to wander back to her surroundings and the information she could recollect from the dark corners of her mind on the strange creatures which live and die in the rainforest. She had read about a twenty-foot man-eating crocodile which could not only creep up on you quietly whilst in the water but could give chase on land offering no mercy. In one book it was said that there are snakes whose venom has no known cure if bitten; pythons as thick as a man's leg and wild pigs with razor sharp tusks that eat anything in their path. But this was not the worst; it was the insects, parasites, viruses and poisonous plants that were the real enemy. Leeches loved the warmth of the tropics and one book graphically detailed how, once full of the victim's blood, they would squirm out of people's pants.

Leeches were not the only Draculas of the forest, mosquitoes, sand flies and elephant flies fed lavishly on the thick, red, juicy human blood. Even worse were the tiny red ticks, looking like sprinkled red powder, that bore their heads into the backs of the knees, the upper thigh and the armpits, causing electrical shocks every time they were touched. Sand fleas, which, if you walked barefoot, would bury themselves deep under your skin to lay eggs. Then there were the wolf spiders and large, hairy, black tarantula-looking creatures that lay in wait for their prey clinging to their tough sticky threads.

Megan could barely move for fear of meeting any of these creatures but eventually exhaustion took over and she fell asleep.

Chapter 3

Old Men of the Forest

Megan woke up with a start. Outside she could hear a man chanting, and then crashing of branches followed by a soft low rumbling sound.

Scrambling to her feet, she tiptoed to the edge of the cave and peered out. There, she saw a group of orang-utans surrounding a tall spindly man wearing a Hard Rock Café T-shirt faded by many years from the burning sun, and his makeshift wheelbarrow. He emptied the wheelbarrow of its contents providing a feast for the orang-utans: bananas, pineapples, durian, rambutan and purple mangosteen to mention just a few.

She then watched him bend down and scoop up a baby orang-utan holding it cupped in his arms, gently stroking its coarse dark ginger hair, singing quietly whilst the mother just watched placidly and ate the welcome fruit. There was an invisible bond between the man and these human-like creatures. What appeared to be coldness by the mother was just a simple acceptance of his presence without the social niceties and a quiet understanding of each other. Words were not necessary, everything that was communicated was done silently.

Setting the baby orang-utan down gently, he counted the heads to check that they were all there, then turned and disappeared into the green blanket of vegetation without a backward glance, still singing.

Megan took this chance to creep noiselessly closer to the orang-utans. She could now see how hairy they were with long arms that dangled to their knees and short legs compared to their bodies. Their faces, palms and soles of their feet were hairless, so too were their ears which nestled deep amongst the hair on their head. Although they seemed to look the same, Megan realised, on closer inspection, that each one had an identifying feature. Some were darker, whilst others had wider faces or exceptionally down-turned mouths. Megan was amazed to see how long and delicate their fingers appeared to be as they prised open the fruit.

The young orang-utan, who, only moments earlier, had been in the clutches of the faded T-shirt man, boldly moved towards her. Reaching out carefully to touch her colourful baseball boots, the baby orang-utan gently ran a finger down the material, fascinated by the colours. Megan sat still and smiled down at the confident little creature that shared her inquisitive characteristic. Pulling the laces, the orang-utan was surprised when they moved. Startled by it, she ran squealing to the security of her mother.

This time the mother turned and stared without emotion in Megan's direction. She ambled over and carefully studied her face. She lifted her hair and peered inside her ears, prised open her mouth and then rifled through her hair. Obviously satisfied, she sat down leaning hard against Megan.

'Wow! What a lump you are!' exclaimed Megan. The orang-utan ignored the insult and continued noisily eating her meal.

The baby, still clinging to its mother, stared suspiciously at Megan in case she had any more moving parts up her sleeve. This time the baby wasn't taking any chances.

The orang-utan offered the remains of the half-eaten fruit to Megan; it was then that she felt incredibly hungry. After all, she hadn't eaten for, yes how many hours had she not eaten? Megan had no idea how much time had passed since she slipped out of the house.

With Megan lost in her thoughts, the orang-utan stood up and wandered off, expertly climbed the nearest tree with her baby attached and disappeared; leaving the rest munching their way through the fruit. Megan felt the loss of her closeness but hunger took over from these emotions.

Suddenly, a fight broke out between three of the remaining baby orang-utans. The squealing was ear piercing. Two of the orang-utans set upon a smaller one chasing it till it vanished and all that was left were their squealing still ringing in her ears plus a few adults that hadn't finished their meal. This episode upset her and it was then that she reached for her piccolo, an automatic reaction to calm herself down. This was something she always turned to when everything became too stressful. Closing her eyes, she began to play and when she opened them again she realised she had become the centre of attention. Those that had left had returned and those that had remained now turned to stare at her. All eyes where upon her. Eating had stopped. Chewing had ceased. The silence was disturbing. One by one they became mesmerized by the music. And then, as suddenly as they'd stopped, they ran for the trees, racing back up to the tops, screaming and scattering in all different directions.

'I know my playing isn't great but I didn't think it was that bad,' remarked Megan despondently.

The magical experience sat warm in Megan's heart and the need to spend more time with them became immensely strong. The orang-utans offered understanding without judgement and an acceptance without her having to obey all the social norms.

Megan, lost in her thoughts, picked up the piccolo and started to play again. It was then that she had this intense feeling of being watched by hundreds of eyes and that the forest around her was moving. Emerging from the thick vegetation were ghost-like creatures. Tall lean men, covered with white paint. Their eyes black and unblinking, jaws set and anger fixed on their painted faces. Megan couldn't believe how stupid she had been by leaving the cave.

One of them started to shout. Two of the other men ran towards her, grabbed an arm each and ran back into the forest followed by the rest of the group. The speed they propelled her at was unnatural. She struggled to stay on her feet as the ground was uneven and low branches reached out and scraped her face and snagged her clothes.

Then, suddenly, they emerged from the trees into sunlight. Tired, scratched and confused Megan was thrown down into the centre of the clearing. There was a lot of shouting between the tribesmen, the women and children looked on in horror. Megan desperately looked around for the children she had met on the riverbank and with relief saw them but they stared like everyone else, refusing to recognise or acknowledge her.

Everyone was shouting; one of the younger men snatched her piccolo; nobody seemed to be in control until a very old man staggered over, leaning heavily on his ornate walking stick. Megan had seen one of those sticks before in a book: it signified power and leadership so she assumed that he was the tribal elder.

'Diro and Sugito, take her to the hut and lock her in,' he said in a very low, controlled voice.

Two of the younger tribesmen picked Megan up and dragged her to a small wooden hut balanced on spindly legs and threw her in. The door banged closed behind her.

Although Megan's view was obscured, she could just make out what was happening through a crack in the slats. And within this group of ghost-like men, her fate was being decided.

The shouting subsided as the village tribesman raised his stick. Without a word, a circle was formed.

'Who is she?' the tribal elder enquired.

'We found her casting a magic spell on the orang-utans,' said the most aggressive tribesman.

'What proof do you have of this, Faisa?'

'I have this,' he said pulling Megan's piccolo out producing what he thought was the evidence to prove Megan's witchcraft.

'Bring it to me.' The old man turned it around in his hand several times. 'How did she use it?'

'By blowing into it to make a hypnotic sound.'

'We saw all the orang-utans being hypnotised,' announced one of the other men.

'Play it for me!' ordered the chief.

As hard as Faisa blew, no sound would come out.

'There,' he said, 'only the spell-caster can make the sound. She has come to kidnap the orang-utans, she must be punished.'

There was a lot of mumbling in agreement from the other tribesmen. One of the younger tribesmen stood up.

'How is this proof, Faisa? You cannot throw a spear as well as me but that does not make me a caster of spells.'

'Sit down, Sugito,' commanded the old man.

Sugito boldly continued, knowing this could put his life in danger. 'But we cannot condemn her for being a spell-caster without more evidence.'

'I said sit down,' repeated the old man a little more sternly.

This time Sugito sat down, after all it was not wise to disobey the village elder.

'We must vote on this. Should she be put to death for being a spell-caster or do we let her go and risk tragedy being brought to our village and our forest?' declared the old man. 'This is for you to decide.' He continued, 'We will meet later when the sun has gone down behind the trees and the stars have filled the dark void.'

And as quietly as they had formed the circle, the men stood up and left.

All Megan could do now was wait.

It was at this point that Megan felt despair; she was pretty sure she had very few allies amongst the tribesmen. Her days were numbered, that was certain, but by how many she did not know.

Day turned into night, the fires were lit and the circle of men resumed.

This, thought Megan, is when I get to hear about my fate. Surely I will wake up soon and find out that I've been dreaming.

This, however, was not to be. Megan was very much awake.

But before the meeting started a tall recognisable figure entered the circle and sat to the right of the old man, Megan sat motionless.

'It couldn't be, surely it couldn't be. How did he get here?'

Chapter 4

Escape is the Only Way Out

'Thaddeus, welcome to our meeting, my trusted friend.' The old man stood up and greeted the bookseller.

'It is an honour as usual to be a part of your illustrious ceremony.'

'Ceremony!' exclaimed Megan to no one in particular.

The food was brought out by the women and handed to each tribesman. There was much chatter and laughter.

From behind the door, Megan heard someone talking to her guard then the door was flung open. There stood Hintu. Relief flooded over Megan, a friendly face at last.

'Ssshhh! It's safer for both of us if you pretend not to know me,' he whispered. 'I'll explain later, be patient.'

He placed the rice and an unrecognisable meat in front of her then walked out without another word. Megan looked at the food and ate it quickly before someone came in to take it away from her.

During the dinner, the bookseller sat next to the old man and talked quietly, not giving Megan a chance to hear what was being said. All she could see was that the old man looked very angry. This didn't help Megan's cause.

Once the eating ceased, the meeting started. Silence hung heavily over the circle. It wasn't until the old man raised his hand that he spoke.

'I asked you all to search inside your soul to decide whether we should kill our captive to protect our village and forest or release her to a fate about which we know not what. What say you?'

'We cannot make a decision with so little evidence. We must ask her into the circle and at least give her a chance to answer our questions,' Sugito argued.

The bookseller whispered something into the old man's ear.

'No,' shouted the old man. 'She will not be allowed to enter the circle, it is forbidden.'

Sugito sat down knowing that he could not win this battle, tradition was too strong to break. For as long as Sugito could remember, women were not allowed to enter the circle; it was only the men, who had proved their hunting skills, that could take part in council meetings.

Megan was furious with the bookseller. He seemed to have a power and an influence over the old man, why didn't he use it to help her? She knew he was probably angry with her for disobeying him but that didn't mean she should die for one small mistake.

'You all know what to do; if you think she should die then bring your voting stick and place it in front of me.'

Megan held her breath. No one moved. There was hope. And then Faisa got up and put his stick down, this started a cascade of votes. One by one each tribesman stood up and placed the stick down in front of the old man. Megan couldn't believe the injustice. Her whole life had been the same: rejected by her parents, rejected by the other children and now rejected by people who didn't even know her name. Another piece inside her died and it was as if someone had drained the final remains of her confidence. A wave of despair swept over her, consuming all her feelings. She felt the lump in her throat restricting her breathing. The tears that she had kept back for so many years silently flowed over her cheeks.

All she could do was lie down and let the grief and loneliness come out. Eventually, Megan cried herself to sleep: a sleep engulfed in nightmares.

'Wake up, wake up, Megan.' It was Hintu tapping gently on the back of the hut.

'You've got to escape.'

'But where do I go?' Megan asked instantly waking up.

'Don't worry about that I can take you to a safe place but you must be ready tomorrow night.' With that he disappeared as quietly as he had come.

Lying awake, Megan reflected on her life and hoped that she would survive this ordeal. What didn't kill her made her stronger or that was what she was hoping would happen. She stayed awake so long that she became aware that light was starting to seep into the hut. Unbeknown to her, this new day was to bring an even greater disaster.

Chapter 5

Hidden Away

'They're not there, they're not there!'

Hearing the shouting, Megan stood up and looked through the slats, she could see the Hard Rock Café T-shirt man running round the village like some crazed lunatic.

'They've gone, what am I to do?' Hopelessness was written over his face.

At first the villagers were as confused as Megan, trying to work out who had gone.

'Iola and her baby Iago, have gone, it's all my fault.'

'I told you she was a spell-caster, she has cast a spell on them and now they've disappeared,' accused Faisa.

Oh no, thought Megan. He's talking about the orang-utans.

The men ran back to their huts and grabbed their hunting spears. Back in the clearance the men gathered and, as if they were using mental telepathy because not a word was said between them, they all ran in different directions to seek their forest dependents.

'Megan, you must escape now, the earth gods are angry and so will my fathers be.' Hintu was ripping at a loose slat with urgency. Megan leant down and started to help until there was a space just big enough for her to squeeze through.

'When I say run you run to the east and wait behind the large Kapok tree.' Hintu waited till the women were talking animatedly about the orang-utans' disappearance. 'Run!'

Megan headed for the wall of trees and hid. Her head was throbbing and her knees could barely support her.

It seemed like an age but could have only been minutes before Hintu joined her. Slowly, they crept through the thick jungle: thorns tore at her skin and hair, shredding her bare skin allowing blood to run freely. Her clothes stuck to her from the combination of blood and sweat, which seeped through every pore. The humidity made it difficult to breathe so every step became harder and harder but fear of death was near. This spurred her on. She wondered, not for the first time, what would happen to Hintu if he was caught with her, would he suffer the same fate as her? Her thoughts were interrupted by Hintu.

'We have to go this way because the jungle is thick and nearly impassable for grown-ups, but beware.'

'Beware of what?'

'Spiders, insects, everything small,' snapped Hintu. 'Now be as quiet as possible.'

Megan had one major fear in life and that was spiders.

'No way, Hintu. I'm not going that way, I'm terrified of spiders.' Megan stood firm and resolute.

Hintu spun round staring her straight in the eyes, 'You have a choice – death or spiders?'

'And that's a choice! Oh well if you put it like that…
aagghh what is happening, my legs are stinging.'
Megan started to jump up and down on the spot.

'Oh no, bullet ants. We should never have stood
still.'

The large black ants had started to crawl up
Megan's trousers and were taking much pleasure
in biting her. It was almost impossible to kill
them, as they seemed to be made of rubber. Hintu
pulled Megan half running half stumbling through
the jungle until they came to a small stream. He
pushed her in and thrust her under the water. The
relief flooded over her but, although the biting had
stopped, she felt that every part of her burned. There
was so much she needed to learn about the dangers
of the rainforest.

Their progress was slow and painful, especially for
Megan. She managed to tear her clothes and add
numerous cuts to her already sensitive skin from the
multitude of thorns.

Hintu suddenly pulled her down and put his finger to his lips. What had he heard? Megan listened hard but still no sound came her way. Then there was a faint snap of a twig and she realised that they had come across one of the tribesmen. Not daring to move they squatted motionless.

Frozen to the spot, Megan saw something out of the corner of her eye hovering just above her shoulder. It was one of those moments when it would have been better not to turn and see what was there, but that goes against human reactions. There, only four centimetres from her shoulder, was a spider the size of a plate, covered in thick black glossy hair and, to Megan, it seemed to be smiling, but that was ridiculous.

It lowered itself down by a sticky thread and, one leg at a time, gently placed itself on her shoulder. Hintu turned and saw Megan paralysed with fear. He grabbed the spider and threw it as far as possible.

'We must move,' he whispered. 'Where there is one, there will be many more. I think my tribesmen have gone so we can start moving but try to make as little sound as possible.' With that he turned and crawled away.

The ground was riddled with tree roots and vines, the way ahead blocked with plants which stood firm or grabbed out to pull you back into their secret world.

Just as Megan thought that every ounce of will and strength had left her body, Hintu stood tall and turned to smile. 'Da daaa!' he announced. There in the clearing was a wooden hut similar to the one that had imprisoned her, standing proudly on stilts.

'We're here, at last. It is not much but it's home for the night.'

'Where is here?' she looked at him in desperation but all he did was turn and walk hastily towards the hut. 'OK, it doesn't matter; I'm too tired to care anyway.' Megan said to herself. 'You were going to tell me why it was safer for you not to know me,' Megan said to Hintu.

'Yes I was, but not just yet. Let's collect firewood and find something to eat before it gets dark. I have to go fairly soon otherwise the villagers will become suspicious, but I'll come back tomorrow,' promised Hintu.

He seemed to be at one with the rainforest, he knew the right plants to eat and the ones which were poisonous. He showed Megan where to collect drinking water and how to start a fire without matches. Quietly, she watched this boy, who worked in harmony with his environment. When he'd finished, he looked at her instinctively knowing what she was thinking.

'I've lived here all my life We must be at one with the rainforest otherwise we'll die.' He looked around the forest and added, 'This is all I know.'

'How do you do that?' questioned Megan.

'What?'

'Know what I'm thinking.'

'We practise sitting still and just listening, it allows us to hear the torment or joy of the spirit and hear the words of the mind.'

'I promised,' he continued, 'to explain why Cayru and I were reluctant to acknowledge you. If someone is accused of being a spell-caster, or witch in your terms, then all their friends and acquaintances, by association, are also spell-casters and would suffer a similar punishment. If they find me here, then I will be put to death too. The only way you can escape death by the hands of my people is to prove your innocence, which will be very difficult. Probably impossible, especially as a girl. I must leave you now.' And with that he ran back into the rainforest and disappeared like the moon behind a cloud.

'How am I ever going to prove my innocence?' Megan said out loud without meaning to. She stared into the fire and tried to see or rather feel the comfort and companionship she had felt with the orang-utans. What she didn't understand was why there was so much panic when Iola and Iago did not come for their food.

Chapter 6

Iola and Iago

After a fitful night sleep, Megan was relieved to see Hintu and Cayru arrive very early in the morning carrying a bowl of food. It wasn't her usual toast and marmalade but at this point Megan would have eaten anything.

'Good morning, Megan. Did you sleep well?' little Cayru enquired airily.

'As much as I could.'

'Cayru and I have been talking. We will help you clear your name but you must answer a question first. Agreed?'

'Agreed.'

'What confuses us is how you got here. There is no evidence of a kayak and you certainly seem very ignorant about the rainforest's ways which means you could not have survived the walk on your own.'

'If I could explain and make it sound true, I would but believe me I have no idea.'

'Try us,' said Cayru. 'We are not so ignorant to the world.'

With some thought, Megan finally answered. 'OK, I will tell you what I know but I cannot explain why.' Megan went on to describe the move to her new house, finding the street where the bookshop was and how she had discovered an unusual atlas. She wasn't too sure whether she should include the part the book-seller played, and for now, she remained cautious, keeping some parts of the story hidden. She had learnt that sometimes it is better to keep things back.

To Megan's amazement, they didn't seem surprised or disbelieving. This encouraged her but also made her nervous getting the feeling that they knew something she didn't. For many minutes after she'd finished, they sat quietly.

Suddenly, Hintu jumped up.

'OK,' he said. 'I don't understand why but I do believe you're telling the truth.' He turned to Cayru who nodded in agreement.

Megan whispered a quiet prayer of thanks.

'Now it's our turn,' Hintu announced. 'Our tribe, the Manyaks, have lived here for many years and lived alongside the many animals that share the rainforest such as the tiger, rhino and elephant but the orang-utans are particularly special to us. We have come to know them and they us. It was decided, many ancestors ago when many orang-utans nearly starved to death, that we would help them when food was scarce. Unfortunately, other men came, men who were not from our tribe and they did not care for our ways and traditions. They do not live in harmony with the rainforest they came to bleed our home dry of all its resources. What they want is the land to grow crops, crops which you cannot eat. We do not understand this.' Hintu shook his head in misery.

'To clear the land,' Cayru continued, 'they cut the big trees to sell them or burn the forest and with it our home. After that they plant trees of the same species in rows upon rows latticing the countryside. These trees offer no food or homes for the orang-utans. The farmers fear them so they are shot leaving many orphaned baby orang-utans.'

Cayru sat silent for a while mustering up the strength to go on. Tears started to stream down her cheeks. 'The father of Iola was searching for some-where to live but sadly came across a group of farmers. It was late in the day and they had been drinking, drinking a lot, and thought it was funny to douse him in petrol and set light to him. He died in agony.' Cayru couldn't continue the story. The pain was too deep, too excruciating, and too heartbreaking. Hintu placed an arm around his sister, tears filling the rim of his eyes too.

'We are a lone voice, we shout but no one hears us,' said Hintu. 'Now it's time to fight back.'

There was a long silence and Megan knew that she should wait quietly for them to finish.

'The men hunt the orang-utans, they choose a mother with a baby clinging to her and kill her to get to the baby,' Hintu went on to explain. 'One day I saw some men shoot a mother orang-utan. The baby was still clinging to her when she fell to the ground. It took two men to pull the distraught baby from the dead mother. It was the baby's face that still haunts me. She cried out and wept for the loss of her mother. The men didn't care, they just threw her into a small wooden crate, clamped it shut and drove off with her in the back of their van.'

'Why?'

'Because they sell them to foreign zoos or private collectors for a high price or,' Hintu paused, 'they keep them as sport.'

'Sport? What do you mean?'

'They are tortured.' Cayru had to finish as Hintu was, by then, choking on his tears. 'The tribe think you were sent by these men to charm them with your music and that they would have only sent a spell-caster to do their dirty work. We don't believe that but our fathers do.'

'They want to kill you in revenge for their lost friends, which there have been many,' Hintu said.

'Show me where these men live,' said Megan.

Cayru and Hintu looked at each other and wordlessly seemed to come to a decision. They had this amazing ability to talk without saying a single word. Cayru walked over to Megan and reached out her hand. This single act of friendship gave Megan the first insight in to what it was like to have someone not reject her.

Megan knew she had to clear her name but more importantly she wanted to help search for Iola and Iago, if they had been taken then their future was going to be unpleasant, very unpleasant. In fact it was not going to be a life at all.

Their journey took them back into the thick rain-forest; not somewhere Megan wanted to return to, but she knew it was the only way. The air inside the forest was heavy, the humidity was intense, and far below the tree canopy the wind was silent. No light penetrated the forest floor making it difficult to navigate despite being midday.

Eventually, they joined a path making it easier to walk. Megan was still sore from the journey the day before but she was determined not to make a fuss as they had risked their lives for her and now it was her turn to return the trust.

Ahead, Megan saw Cayru stop abruptly and bend down. She was studying something. When Megan caught up with her, she realised with horror what Cayru was looking at. It took a while to recognise the burnt body lying at the side of the road but she knew with certainty that this was the body of the missing orang-utan, Iola.

Nobody spoke, nobody could. The world seemed to have stopped turning; time was meaningless and a wave of sheer hopelessness swept over Megan. She then heard Cayru sobbing quietly next to her, so she reached out to hold her hand tightly trying desperately not to cry herself.

'The bad men must have Iago but the question is what are they going to do with her?' Hintu looked at both the girls seeming to look deep into their minds.

'Do you have the courage to go on, Megan?'

She didn't know how to answer him. She knew she wasn't particularly brave and she also knew he had seen that in her.

'There is only one way Hintu, and that is forward.' Megan tried to sound convincing but she knew he had seen deep into her soul.

He nodded and gently placed his hand on her shoulder.

'Thank you,' he said.

After many hours of fighting their way through the forest, Hintu stopped and lay down. Quietly calling them over, he indicated for them to lie down too. Through the gaps in the leaves, they could see a camp made up of a few very basic mud huts – it was the loggers' camp. But it was not the camp that made Megan weep inside but what she saw beyond that.

Where the forest had been, nothing remained. There was only the grey naked earth with small black head-stones pushing up through the ground. Smoke swirled round the headstones giving Megan the feeling of being in some horror movie. When she looked harder, she real-ised that what appeared to be headstones was actually a vast desert of short sharp burnt tree stumps covered in a grey ash. This pitiful view reached for miles into the horizon: thousands of acres of land had been deforested. Only a small pocket of forest remained close to the camp.

'This is what they will do to our land soon, which means we will have to move on.'

'But you must be able to do something,' Megan exclaimed, feeling frustrated and angry.

'Like what? I told you we have no voice; only money speaks here. Nobody cares what happens to our people.'

Huddled in a corner of the camp, a group of men were laughing and from the middle of the group the children could hear a scream of sheer panic.

'Oh no, it is Iago,' said Cayru.

The pain of Iago's torment was obviously too much for Cayru and she suddenly burst out from their hiding place and ran towards the group of men. Megan was about to follow but Hintu pulled her down.

'That's typical of Cayru; she always rules her life with her heart. There's nothing we can do on our own against these men, we're no use to Iago and Cayru if we show ourselves now.'

'But we can't leave Cayru,' Megan pressed.

'We must and we just have to hope she'll be alright. We must wait for dark.'

Before they retreated into the forest they watched with shock as Cayru tried to beat one of the men. He lifted her easily into the air and dangled her upside down from her ankle.

'What do we have here? It looks like one of those jungle people we're trying to get rid off. Well maybe we should do ourselves a favour and start with this one,' the man holding her said. 'Why don't we lock her up in the toilet with the orang-utan until we decide what to do with them both. Maybe we could sell both of them to the zoo.'

The other men laughed.

The man carried her and Iago to a small wooden toilet, only big enough for two people to stand up in, and threw them in unceremoniously, slamming the door shut and bolting it from the outside.

A voice from one of the other men made Hintu more alert.

'What if there are more hiding in the forest? I think we should have a look.'

Hintu and Megan saw the group of men stand up and walk towards them. Without a word to each other they started to quietly crawl back into the forest. When they felt they had gone far enough

back, they stood up and ran through the tangled bushes. Megan spied a small opening to a cave and pointed to it silently. They both had to lie flat on their bellies to squeeze inside.

After a few minutes, they could hear the heavy trampling of the men heading towards them. Blood ran cold through Megan's veins and the hairs on the back of her neck stood on end. She tried to calm her breathing but the more she tried, the louder it seemed to get. From the cave, they could see a pair of thick black boots standing outside the entrance. All he needed to do was bend down and peer inside the cave to discover them.

To their relief they heard another of the men calling.

'There is no one here or if there was, they've gone. I'm not wasting any more time, we have a job to do.'

With that the black boots turned and tramped away.

The children waited until dark lying in silence till Hintu decided it was time to go.

'So exactly how are we going to rescue them?' Megan asked.

'We are going to sneak in and take them with us.'

'And that is your plan?' Megan retorted.

'Unless you have something better it's the only one we have,' Hintu snapped. 'I suppose you are planning to stay out of this one,' he continued.

Megan was angry with him, at no time had she said that she wouldn't help. She refused to answer and just marched off in the direction of the men's camp.

Why did she feel guilty, why did she feel that Cayru's capture was her fault? After all, she didn't ask to come to this gloomy place, nor had she been a part of Iola's death and nor did she encourage Cayru to run off into the middle of the loggers' camp. She felt that again disaster just followed her around and everyone seemed to think it was her fault.

They crouched down at the edge of the camp and waited for a long time before the men drank themselves to sleep. When the snoring from the camp was louder than the noises from the forest, Hintu and Megan crept into the camp to where Iago and Cayru were being held.

Megan kept a lookout while Hintu slid back the bolt of the wooden door with as much care as possible, only to be confronted with a smell making him jerk back with disgust. The toilet consisted of a raised wooden plank; in the centre was a hole which led into a pit of human faeces. Clutching Cayru's arms was Iago, small and very frightened.

Cayru couldn't see who was there so cowered further back for fear that one of the men had decided what they were going to do with them.

'Cayru,' Hintu whispered, 'let's go.'

She jumped into Hintu's arms and sobbed.

'We must go quickly.'

Just as they started to make a dash for the cover of the forest, one of the men, half-drunk and half-asleep, walked towards the toilet. He tripped over a man who'd fallen asleep where he'd been sitting the night before.

'Hey watch where you're going!'

'Stupid place to sleep,' the walking man replied.

'Did you call me stupid?'

'Yes I did.'

With that he dragged himself to standing and hit the man hard on the nose. The other man flew back and landed on a very surprised Megan.

'Run!' Hintu shouted as loud as he dare.

Everyone ran except Megan who was trapped by the man with the newly broken nose. She felt the warm sticky blood trickle down her face and tried to pull away but he was too quick for her. Grabbing her arm, he pulled her up and dragged her towards the toilet. He roughly hurled her in and slammed the door shut throwing the bolt across. She then heard him going to the toilet right outside.

He shouted to the man who'd hit him to bring a chain and padlock. Wrapping the chain around tightly, he padlocked her into the toilet.

She couldn't see her new gaol but she could certainly smell it.

Megan's captor raised the alarm to the semi-conscious men.

'The orang-utan and the girl have escaped,' he shouted urgently. 'Quick, wake up, you lazy louts, we've got to catch them.'

Bleary-eyed and still half asleep, the men jumped up and ran off in different directions. Then returned realising that no plan had been put in place.

'What shall we do?' asked one of the now more alert men.

It was this confusion and bad planning that allowed Hintu, Cayru and Iago time to escape.

Chapter 7

Animal Talk

Megan slumped hopelessly against the rough wooden door and moved from semi-wakefulness to a sleep full of nightmares. She wasn't sure how long this went on for but she gradually became aware of shafts of light streaming through the multitude of gaps in the walls. A wave of nausea washed over her as she inhaled the pungent smell of the open-drop toilet. She felt like she had landed in a sewage tank without coming up smelling of roses.

Engine noises fired up all around her, men were shouting abuse to each other and then she could hear the awful noise of trees creaking as they were lifted up by the roots and levered out of the ground then dumped callously in a pile of burning wood. More rainforest was being destroyed.

Once gone it will never be the same. Thousands of animals will be left with no homes, unable to find food. Man's greed for land to make money was insatiable. There seemed to be no end to the destruction and, unless action was taken immediately, no rainforest would be left; with it we would lose plants, which could heal, and animals that give use so much pleasure. Many more species will become extinct and future generations will just have pictures to remind them of these majestic and remarkable creatures. We lost the dodo and didn't learn from that. We have lost three species of tiger and still haven't learnt from that yet we continue to destroy. How many other animals will become extinct before we finally learn the lesson?

'Surely we're supposed to share this planet with all the species, not destroy it!' Megan declared to no one in particular.

No food or water had been forthcoming that morning, she wondered whether the men had forgotten her existence. However, it wasn't long before she realised that this wasn't the case.

From within the remaining forest, Megan heard a deafening commotion. Guns were firing, men were yelling and the high-pitched sound of panic could be heard.

Megan strained to see what was happening through the slats of her confinement. Men were scurrying through the forest, the tops of the trees were swaying and crashing, some men were running in the opposite direction to hide behind the mud huts whilst others were randomly shooting into the sky. All of sudden, one of the men shouted a celebratory whoop and there was a distinct sound of branches breaking and a loud thud.

A few of the men slapped hands and congratulated each other. Megan couldn't work out why they were so happy with themselves. She could see a few of the men carrying a sack, or rather that was what it looked like.

'Put it in the toilet with the girl!' ordered one of the men. Megan presumed he was their manager.

The padlock was unlocked and the chains slumped to the ground. The bolt was shot back and something very heavy and furry was thrown at her. She very quickly realised that another orang-utan had lost its home, possibly its life. Hauling the creature up, she cradled the orang-utan in her arms. It was then that she felt the sticky liquid on her hands: blood. This beautiful, vulnerable creature had been shot. Megan cried with frustration and hugged the orang-utan, sobbing uncontrollably into the creature's orange fur.

Megan could hear the faint rasping sound of the orang-utan's breathing. It was alive but for how long she didn't know.

'Please help me!'

Startled, Megan looked up. Had she heard that or was that a figment of her imagination?

'Please, I have to find my baby.'

Again Megan looked round to find out where the voice had come from. Glancing down at the orang-utan, she realised that it was coming from this dying animal. Her pleading eyes were boring into Megan's soul.

'I think I've just understood what you are saying but I'm not certain. Either that or I'm going a little insane.'

'You aren't going insane, through your empathy you've learnt to hear me.' The orang-utan seemed to be gaining in strength.

'How can I help you?'

'When I fell, I left my baby at the top of the tree, she will be frightened and uncertain what to do. Please help.'

'There's not a lot I can do, as you can see I'm a prisoner too. I might be human but I'm not like one of them.' Megan pointed towards the workers that were continuing to destroy the natural habitat.

The orang-utan slumped forward and collapsed weakly. Her body was extremely thin and malnourished. With the loss of her land, came with it starvation followed closely by death, which was where this orang-utan was heading quite quickly.

'I will not allow you to die,' Megan cried out determinedly. 'You will not die. I read somewhere that you can heal just with the power of the mind.'

Megan shut her eyes and willed the bleeding to cease. Opening one eye at a time, she glanced hopefully at the orang-utan: still no improvement. 'I'm not giving up just yet.'

The orang-utan's breathing became shallower and slower. Megan was suddenly filled with light and warmth as she placed her hand gently over the wound and willed it to heal.

There was more commotion coming from the forest. Megan knew that they had found the baby. She just hoped that the mother couldn't hear or see what was happening or going to happen to this little innocent and petrified baby orang-utan.

The baby was thrown into a tiny box and the lid hammered down so that escape was impossible.

Megan could hear the whimpering of the baby crying but this soon faded out. Exhaustion had taken its place and the baby had gone quiet. She was worried that it was as emaciated as the mother and if so, she would not have long to live without sustenance.

'My name is Nayla.' A voice came from the darkness.

Megan swung round and saw the orang-utan lifting her head to talk to her.

'Mine is Megan. It's lovely to meet you.' Tears filled her eyes as she saw Nayla attempting to smile but her energy was low.

Just as she was doing this, the door was wrenched open by one of the angry workers. He threw in rice, water and some bananas. Megan lifted the weakened head and began to feed Nayla.

'Thank you, my friend. I shall never forget your act of kindness.'

Nayla fell into a deep sleep. Despite Megan's arm going numb, she continued to hold the stricken animal. To Megan's surprise she began to sing to the sleeping orang-utan a song that her grandmother had sung to her when she was much younger.

She had loved her grandmother deeply. It was her that talked to Megan, listened to her and allowed her to be herself. They would spend hours in the wood collecting and identifying mushrooms, plants and berries. In the evening, her grandmother would read her books and they would talk about their days. Every day with her grandmother was full of fun; laughter was never far from their hearts. Sometimes they would laugh so hard that their cheeks and stomachs would ache. Megan's mother would get very cross with them and ban them from seeing each other, sometimes for days.

The day she found out that her grandmother had died, was the day that a large part of her died too. Her mother didn't seem to care, in fact it was a relief for her. Her grandmother had done and said some very weird things but they made Megan laugh. However, her mother just thought that she was mad. Her father didn't even go to the funeral. As usual, he was 'far too busy with work'.

As Megan's mother was an only child, she inherited her mother's money. It was only after she died that they discovered how rich she really was. Megan's mother immediately spent it, buying a grand house, sports car, ridiculous clothes and having pretentious parties. None of which Megan wanted to have anything to do with. She missed her grandmother more each day and the loneliness swelled up to immense proportions inside of her that she didn't know how to release it.

Nayla stirred briefly, it seemed that every breath was restoring her strength and determination. Eventually, Megan fell into a disturbed sleep. Through the exhausted haze, she could hear crying, squealing, laughing, jeering but she wasn't sure whether it was real or another nightmare.

At some point, Megan must have drifted into a deep sleep because she was woken by a gentle tap on her arm.

'Wake up, Megan!' Nayla ordered urgently. 'We need to talk.'

'About what?'

'We only have a short time for me to tell you my story. I need you to know it so you can share it with your world.'

Megan was trying really hard to concentrate, after so many sleepless nights she was exhausted. Recognising the urgency and importance in Nayla's voice, she sat up to listen intently or as intently as she was physically capable of doing.

'This deforestation has been going on for many years. Too many animals have lost their lives or their habitat. At one point, all the species lived harmoniously with the rainforest; it gave to us and we gave to it. For our ancestors, the rainforest was their world and it provided food all year round. You must realise Megan, that orang-utans live in trees and some never come to the ground. They eat, sleep and feed at the top of the trees. We thought we were safe until the machines came. They recklessly destroyed everything in their path. We tried to move further back but the machines were relentless. They constantly pursued us deeper and deeper into the forest. Every day we woke up to find more of our land had been destroyed.

'When I was only four months old, my mother was killed by a machete. I tried to run but baby orang-utans could be sold as pets and the men were fast. Money was exchanged and from then on, I lived the next eight years of my life in a small cage. As I grew bigger, the cage grew smaller to a point where I had to lean over as there was not enough room for me to stand upright. If I stood in the middle of the cage, I could touch all four corners.

'I'd never climbed a tree before and didn't know the plants to eat. You see, in our world we stay with our mother till we are six years old. They teach us everything we need to know to survive on our own.

'It must have just been pure luck but one day one of the humans forgot to lock the padlock. I took this opportunity to escape. Despite my new-found freedom, I was still a prisoner really. I didn't know how to feed myself or make a nest in the trees or how to climb a tree. This was when luck came my way.

'I was found at the side of the road half-starved; by then my ribs were sticking out through my bare leathery skin: my previous captors had thought it funny to shave my head and body, leaving me bald and uncomfortable.

'I was bundled into a box, by now I was too exhausted to care any more. When I woke up, I found myself in paradise. There was food all around me, other orang-utans were playing close by – they seemed very happy – and best of all, there was no cage.

'I lived there for many years and the humans taught me the right plants to eat, how to build a nest and how to climb trees. I gained confidence and strength. Then came the unhappy day that I had to leave them. I understood why but I really didn't want to go, I knew what a terrible world there was out there.

'Over the years I began to love my new environment until it started all over again. The men came and the land was cleared. You know the rest.'

Nayla fell into a silent reflection. Sadness cloaked her like a blanket. Megan didn't dare to move.

'Right, out you come!' The door was wrenched open and one of the workers yanked Megan out by the wrist. She had just enough time to look back and catch the fear in Nayla's eyes.

Chapter 8

A Magical Escape

They bound Megan's hands and feet tightly, pushed her to the ground and started shouting questions at her. They weren't really interested in the answer as there was no space between each question to allow her to answer, so Megan just remained silent.

Finally, one of the men came over untied her hands and passed her some more rice and bananas, ordering the men to stop. Megan saw in his eyes an element of humanity but he was only one of the seven men.

Later that night, the men were sitting round the fire drinking and arguing – again. They had rebound her hands but had failed to imprison her in the toilet as they thought she was harmless, but that decision proved to be a big mistake.

She was seething inside; fury coursed through her veins and she wanted justice. Justice for Iola and justice for all the other orang-utans. She wished wholeheartedly that she had the power to do something.

She stared at a plank wishing she could pick it up and whack them on the back of the head with it. To her surprise the plank started to wobble. Megan thought she was seeing things. She stared intently at it again – the plank lifted just a little bit more off the ground. Staring at it with even greater force, the plank really did lift up in the air and float about a foot off the ground.

'Hey, what's going on?'

Megan jumped and the plank crashed to the ground. All the men looked round to see what had happened. They were still a little jumpy after the orang-utan episode earlier; they were paranoid that another one would emerge from the forest.

*

When Megan realised that it wasn't her he was talking to, she returned her focus to the plank. One unwary worker had wandered off to the forest outskirts to go to the toilet. Megan trained the plank to float quietly over to him and hover just behind his head. Releasing all her willpower on him, the plank whacked him really hard on the back of the head. He stumbled forward and crumpled uncomplainingly to the ground.

'One down, six more to go,' Megan mumbled.

The men continued to drink until they tipped over the edge from sobriety to insobriety – yes they were completely drunk. This was going to be to Megan's advantage. This was when it all kicked off.

Glass bottles came flying towards them and pieces of lit firewood jumped in front of the faces of the now terrified men, causing chaos. The men scattered in all directions but, in hot pursuit, were some lorry tyres. The tyres chased the men until they trapped them inside, pinning their arms to their sides. The tyres started to roll off in different directions across the cleared but very bumpy land with the men squeezed inside. All Megan could hear were the cries for help fading into the distance.

'Help? You must be joking!'

Megan willed the knife over to cut the ropes. Once free, she ran over to the toilet to release Nayla, who was exhausted by now. Megan lifted her out as gently as possible but with as much as speed as she could. Desperately, she looked round for something to transport her in and found a wheelbarrow.

'Needs must…' Megan observed.

Dumping its contents, she placed Nayla inside with as much reverence as was possible considering the indignation of being slumped inside a wheelbarrow. She then concentrated on finding the baby.

Panic and fear were a constant companion but she felt a huge responsibility to help another creature. The campsite had been plunged into darkness as the only light available had been the fire and she had, after all, used it to scare the men away. She stumbled her way round the campsite until she found the small box with the baby in.

Picking it up, she now had the added problem of finding the wheelbarrow again. In her panic mode, she hadn't clocked the direction she'd wandered off in.

'Nayla, where are you?' Megan called out hoping that Nayla would have some energy to reply.

'Nayla, call to me, help me find you again. I have your baby, you need to live for her.'

There was a faint, low rumbling sound at first but this was replaced with the sound of a howl; a howl of pain, a howl of frustration but most of all a howl of sheer determination.

'That's it, my friend, keep going.'

Megan picked her way between the fallen bottles and debris left from the chaos and followed the sound to the wheelbarrow. She yanked open the small box and retrieved the painfully thin baby. Megan gently placed the baby with her mum who, despite the baby's frail body, clung desperately to her mother.

Even though Megan was exhausted, from somewhere deep down, she found the strength needed to make their escape. She pushed the two orangutans along the cleared paths that stretched for many miles. She couldn't believe the amount of forest that had been destroyed. It was now that she had time to wonder why they were clearing the land. She was determined, if she ever made it home, to discover what was happening. What did they grow on those trees that was so important to the world?

After traipsing across deep ruts and felled trees, Megan finally reached the edge of the rainforest. They continued their journey deeper into the forest. Before the light vanished, she found a clearing to set up camp. Carefully, she took both orang-utans out of the wheelbarrow and lay them on the floor. Her work was not yet done. Her first job was to collect firewood and food. Megan had watched Hintu when he'd helped her escape and learnt what was edible and what was to be avoided.

Feeling drained, she tried to use her newly found magical powers but they seemed to have vanished.

'Maybe I need to be angry to use them.'

Knowing that spiders and insects, which could kill, lay in wait, Megan braved the dangers of the rainforest and found fruit for herself but more importantly for the two weak creatures that were relying on her.

She fed the two orang-utans first before gorging on a diet of bananas and breadfruit. Nayla seemed to muster some energy but she was still very weak from losing a lot of blood.

With the fire blazing and the sound of the rainforest echoing through her ears, Megan had a chance to replay all the events from the past couple of days. Nayla stirred and hobbled over to join her still hanging on to her weakening baby.

'Thank you, my friend. I owe you my life.' Nayla rested a hand over hers and leant her head on Megan's shoulder. This was a new sensation to Megan, apart from her grandmother, Hintu and Cayru, she'd never known friendship. It felt good.

This was how they were found when the sound of crashing and hollering came through the forest. Startled and confused, both Nayla and Megan tried to run. Nayla shot up a tree with her baby clinging to her, vanishing into the canopy. Megan was not so lucky, she ran straight into the arms of a Manyak. More precisely she ran into Faisa.

Chapter 9

Caught

'Only the guilty run!' barked Faisa as he seized Megan's arm. This really wasn't going well for her.

Faisa dragged her unceremoniously back to the Manyak's village and threw her into one of the wooden huts. Looking up, she saw three women squatting down preparing food. They only gave her a cursory glance before continuing with their daily duties. Not one of them spoke.

The wooden hut was crudely built; it stood on stilts with a bright green, torn plastic lino semi-covering the planked flooring. Chairs had been placed around the outside of the room with gold tinsel wrapped around three pillars which held up the ceiling. Four foam mattresses were stacked in the corner with pillows, sheets and mosquito nets folded up neatly on top.

Latifah, the oldest woman, stood up and wiped her hands on her flowery skirt. She then lit the stove and began to boil some water. Without a word, she made tea and brought a steaming mug over to Megan. When she handed it to her, her deep brown eyes looked hard into Megan's. Not a flicker of emotion crossed Latifah's face. Turning back to her work, she continued kneading the dough.

'Can you tell me if Nayla and her baby are safe?' pleaded Megan. 'She'd been shot by the men, who're destroying the forest, and half-starved. I tried to feed her but she was very weak and I struggled to find enough food. I'm really worried for her safety, particularly her baby.'

Latifah looked up but said nothing.

Megan desperately wanted to ask about Hintu and Cayru but was worried that it would get them into trouble or even more trouble. She had remembered what Hintu had said about those who were associated with spell-casters and decided that silence was more prudent and definitely safer for Hintu and Cayru.

Megan sighed loudly and lay down on the lino. Latifah came over and placed a pillow under her head and gently stroked her face. A tear started to roll down Megan's face, it had all been too much. Not wanting Latifah to see, she rolled over and allowed the tears to just come. She was too exhausted to care any more: sleep and food had not been plentiful and this was starting to take its toll on Megan's morale and energy.

She must have fallen asleep because, when she awoke, the room was empty and darkness had descended. She could hear a heated discussion going on beyond the window. Despite feeling very groggy, she knew the discussion had to be about her therefore it was important to focus on what was being said.

'Why did she run if she isn't guilty?' Faisa questioned the council.

'Wouldn't you if you had a death sentence hanging over your head and no way of clearing your name?' retorted Sugito. He continued, 'We need a fairer way to try her.'

Megan scanned the circle of men and saw the familiar shape of the bookseller.

'Him again!' exclaimed Megan.

'May I speak?' the bookseller asked reverentially.

'Thaddeus you are our honoured guest and an honest person, you may speak,' answered the village elder. The ornate talking stick was placed in front of Thaddeus permitting him to continue speaking.

'Let us find Nayla and her baby. Let them tell their story. We can continue arguing till dawn but it will be no good as none of us know the truth.'

Silence hung over the circle momentarily. It was hard advice to ignore.

'No!' exclaimed Faisa.

'Faisa, be quiet!' ordered the village elder. 'Thaddeus has given us good guidance, I agree with it. We now

need to vote on it.' Turning to the rest of the men, the village elder asked, 'If you think we should find Nayla and her baby before casting a judgment, then place your voting stick in the circle.'

No one moved.

Defiantly, Sugito stood up and placed his in the centre. No one else moved. The men looked at each other all waiting to see what the others would do. Many of the men were frightened of Faisa, he was a very powerful man and wouldn't forget anybody who had defied him.

Once, one of the younger council members, Kenji, spoke out against Faisa in front of a few men. This had incensed him. Faisa vowed to take revenge. He waited for that time to come and when it did Kenji only just survived the ordeal. When they were out hunting, Faisa contrived to be on his own with Kenji. He crept up behind him and knocked him out. Faisa then staked him to a tree to die slowly. No one knew what had happened to Kenji. In the village's eyes, he had simply disappeared. Luckily, after a few days one of the children found and released him. It took many months for Kenji to recover from the snake and insect bites and the trauma of the event. He became introverted and didn't join in council meetings or participate in the hunts. Eventually, the village elder became frustrated with him and banished him from the village, ordering him to live alone in the rainforest. From that day to this no one had seen or heard from him.

Slowly but surely, some of the men brought their voting sticks to the centre of the circle.

'Is that it?' demanded the tribal leader. 'Diro count the sticks.'

Fourteen votes had been cast and there were twenty-eight men eligible to vote – women had no say in this world. It all rested on the decision of the village elder. He seemed to look into the darkness, searching for a decision. He appeared to be silently communicating to someone, someone who was just out of sight. Megan looked hard into that darkness and could make out the small figure of Latifah. Her eyes blazed. It was at that moment that Megan knew she was the real leader. The woman behind the great tribal leader. She was his voice of reason, of common sense.

'Put my voting stick into the circle, Diro,' demanded the village elder.

With this final action, Faisa stormed out of the circle swearing revenge.

The tribal leader hung his head in shame and wondered what he had done to have such an angry son.

Chapter 10

Missing

Iago clung to Cayru as they traipsed through the remaining rainforest towards their home. They had to get help although they weren't convinced the tribal men would risk their own lives to help Megan.

'We must return Iago first,' Cayru said.

Despite their concern for Megan, Cayru and Hintu knew their priority was to get Iago as far away from the forest workers as possible. They had heard that baby orang-utans were worth a lot of money in the outside world and once she was gone it would be impossible to rescue her.

'We'll rest here,' Hintu announced. 'It's getting dark and we need to eat and sleep.'

Cayru placed Iago down to help Hintu collect firewood and food from the forest.

'Did you hear that Hintu?' Cayru was suddenly alert.

They both stood silently but no sound could be heard.

'You're imaging things, as usual,' Hintu said dismissively. He never really took Cayru seriously. This made her mad: he was always so superior.

Cayru was sure she could hear the cracking of branches, the rustling of leaves and a low cry but it was very unlikely that other humans would be this far into the rainforest: it was only the Manyak tribe that ventured this far in.

At first when they returned to their makeshift campsite, they didn't notice that something was different. The light had faded rapidly and their concentration was elsewhere. After lighting a fire, Cayru turned her attention to Iago but was horrified to find that she'd gone.

'Where is Iago?' Cayru yelped in panic. 'She's gone!'

Both Cayru and Hintu picked up a burning stick for light and ran through the forest yelling her name but only silence confronted them. She'd vanished into the night. It made no sense. She wouldn't have gone on her own and yet there was no danger from man here.

'What about tigers?' Cayru said thinking of some of the gruesome options that might have befallen Iago. 'You should've listened to me. We should've come back to check she was OK, I knew I could hear something.' Cayru was fuming with Hintu. As well as being angry with Hintu, she knew she had herself to blame for not taking action when she'd heard the sound. She'd sensed that danger was close by and did nothing.

'Aggghhh! I'm so stupid,' she burst out.

With anger still in her heart, she stormed off in the opposite direction. Not a good idea when she knew that an evil spirit was near.

Out of the darkness, a hand grabbed her around the waist and another over her mouth, dragging her roughly back through the forest. She tried to wriggle free but her kidnapper was much stronger than her. She struggled to stay on her feet as she was being dragged backwards rapidly through the forest. Her kidnapper increased the pace and negotiated the thickness of the forest with great deftness, making it difficult for her to keep up.

A branch caught Cayru across the forehead and blood started to trickle down into her eyes leaving her semi-blind. She kept wiping it away but it continued to flow.

After what felt like an age, she was thrown to the ground and a blindfold roughly placed over her eyes. Her hands were tied tightly behind her back and a gag put over her mouth to prevent her from calling out. To add further discomfort, Cayru's abductor tied her tightly to a tree. Desperately, she ran through her head what had happened, and wondered who it could be. But each time she drew a blank.

When the throbbing in Cayru's ears subsided, she could just make out a faint whimpering noise coming from behind her.

She could only guess that Iago was close by and in a similar predicament.

Hintu had heard the commotion but couldn't see what had happened. He called to Cayru – no response was forthcoming.

'Keep calm, Hintu,' he reassured himself even though his voice was trembling. 'What's going on?'

Apart from the cacophony of night sounds in the rainforest, his immediate space was quiet.

Suddenly, a hand reached out to grab him. He struggled and kicked but to no avail, the hands were too strong.

'Be quiet!' Kenji ordered softly. He pulled Hintu to the ground.

Footsteps crept past them, Hintu couldn't see who it was. He didn't know whether the enemy was Kenji or the person creeping past.

Kenji waited quite a while before releasing him.

'What are you doing?' bawled Hintu. 'You scared me half to death. What have you done with Cayru and Iago?'

'Oh dear, I thought that might happen,' uttered Kenji more to himself than Hintu.

Hintu snapped, 'Perhaps you would like to explain more.'

'I haven't got time to explain now because we need to move quickly. You must do as I say without question no matter what you see. Promise me. Promise me!' Kenji barked.

Hintu was a little surprised, he had always known Kenji to be gentle and caring and here he was being hostile and aggressive.

'O-k-a-y...' Hintu stammered.

'Follow me and do what I do, no talking until I say so.'

Silently and obediently, Hintu trailed behind Kenji through the forest until they could see a faint flickering light. As the light neared, Hintu could see a crouching figure and another one slumped against the tree.

Kenji indicated for Hintu to duck down. From the blackness, other figures materialised like ghosts emerging from the mist. They watched as the figures exchanged money for a wooden crate. They slapped each other on the back and then shared a drink or two around the fire. Laughter could be heard weaving its way through the trees and vines. Finally, they left holding the crate and disappeared into the night.

Kenji and Hintu watched the remaining figure go over to the slumped shape by the tree and do something, but they couldn't see clearly what they were doing. Eventually, they moved back to the fire and lay down.

Kenji and Hintu waited a while, giving them time to fall asleep. They watched the fire's embers slowly burn itself out before they made a move. As they crept closer, Hintu realised that it was Cayru leaning against the tree. Impulsively, he jumped up to release her but Kenji caught his wrist.

'Patience – Faisa is a very dangerous man. If he wakes, then your life will not be worth living.'

'Faisa!' Hintu exclaimed. 'Why?'

Kenji wasn't interested in answering; he knew that he had to take this opportunity to rescue Cayru now or it would be too late.

The one thing Manyaks are very proud of is their ability to travel through the forest leaving no trail or making no sound, it was now that this skill became important. Making absolutely no sound, Kenji crept up behind Cayru.

'Please don't make a noise,' he whispered to her. 'We're here to rescue you.'

Kenji cut the ropes and released her. Quietly, they beat a hasty retreat into the forest; vanishing into the dawn light.

With enough distance between Faisa and them, Cayru urgently asked what had happened to Iago.

'What do you mean?' asked Kenji.

'Iago was in the crate.'

Kenji and Hintu looked at each other, both thinking the same thing.

'You two go back to your village,' Kenji ordered.

Hintu was about to protest but he remembered he'd promised to do as he was told without question.

'NOW!' Kenji barked again.

They didn't need to be told twice.

Chapter 11

The Hearing

Cayru and Hintu charged back into the village expecting to be welcomed back but this was not to be the case. According to Manyak laws, if you are in collusion with a criminal, then you are guilty of their crime too.

'Put them with the prisoner,' proclaimed the village elder reluctantly. They were only children but the law applied to everyone and they had deliberately disobeyed it. He knew his wife would be disappointed with him but what could he do? He needed time to think, time to find a sensible solution.

At first, Megan was hugely relieved to see them alive but rapidly realised the situation.

'Oh no, I've done this to you!' Megan hung her head in shame. 'Why can't I get anything right? My parents are correct, I'm useless and always causing trouble.'

'Stop blaming yourself,' Cayru retorted impatiently. 'We made our own decisions knowing the laws. We knew you weren't here to kill or poach the orang-utans and we were standing up for justice. Someone needs to. Our laws need to change and unless we make a stand everything will stay the same.'

'Well said!' Hintu added, surprised and proud of his sister's outcry.

Megan felt a little ashamed of her own self-pitying behaviour.

'What about Iago?'

There was an awkward silence between them. Cayru turned away and intentionally ignored the question. She was unwilling to answer it and so was Hintu but he found the courage from somewhere.

He told her all about the escape, journeying through the forest and then Faisa kidnapping Cayru and Iago. He went on to tell her the bad news about Iago being sold to men; unknown men and it being very unlikely to get her back. They talked late into the night sharing their stories and their emotions that they had gone through. The one thing Megan was reluctant to tell them about was her new found magical abilities. For now, she felt it wiser to keep it quiet. It was, however, a little tricky explaining how she had managed to escape.

From the community circle outside, drums started to play rhythmically but dolefully. Both Cayru and Hintu rushed to the window to watch the hearing. They recognised the beat of the drum and knew what it meant.

Over their shoulder, Megan watched the men appearing from the darkened forest, finding their seats and placing their tribal voting stick in front of them. No one spoke. There seemed to be a heavy atmosphere hanging over the proceedings.

Outside the council circle, Megan noticed a shadowy outline sitting motionless on a rickety

bench to the side of one of the huts. The tribal leader looked across at it and nodded imperceptibly. For what seemed like a fleeting moment, the figure seemed to lose form, shimmer and then vanish. Megan wasn't convinced that what she had seen had actually happened.

'Life takes many twists and turns and this tribe has to follow them,' declared the tribal leader. 'This stranger entered into our village four days ago, we've accused her of luring the orang-utans out of the forest with her music to sell them on for profit and yet we have no evidence.'

'I have evidence!'

Everyone turned to stare at the raised voice of Faisa coming out from amongst the trees.

The three onlookers stared, shocked at his arrival.

'I've witnessed Cayru and Hintu selling Iago to the forest workers. As for the stranger, she has sold Nayla and the baby Lomon. You can search their pockets, you will find money and plenty of it.'

Diro dragged the children into the centre of the circle and emptied their pockets. To their surprise, he found 1000 ringgits.

'But I've... I've... no idea where that came from,' Cayru half stammered, half protested.

'There is your evidence,' Faisa declared pleased with himself.

'Where is the evidence for the stranger?' challenged the tribal leader.

'They must've put all the money together to share it out later.' Faisa seemed to have an answer for everything.

The children tried to protest further but were quickly silenced.

The tribal leader's face paled as the blood drained away. He was tired of this constant bickering and he longed for peace within the village. He yearned to step down and hand over to one of his sons, but Faisa was too unpredictable and caused too much warfare amongst the Manyaks, as for his other son, Kenji, he was sadly lost to him forever.

He had no other option but to set the voting process in action. The voting sticks were placed one by one in the circle. It was a sombre affair and many of the men unwillingly placed their stick down to cast their vote.

Resigned to the decision, the tribal leader ordered for the children to be returned to the hut.

As the children were hauled away, they shouted their protests but it fell on deaf ears.

'How did he get the money into my pocket?' sobbed Cayru.

'He must have slipped it in. Don't blame yourself, you were blindfolded Cayru, and he's clever,' Hintu reassured her.

'Sly you mean,' retorted Cayru.

'What happens now?' asked Megan trying to change the subject.

'You really don't want to know,' Hintu cautioned.

'Try me.'

'We have to tell her,' Cayru pointed out. 'There is a snake called the Banded Sea Krait, whose venom has no known antidote. At first you don't feel anything due to its anaesthetic effect. Then the poison dissolves the muscles leaving you paralysed, next your urine turns a deep red colour and eventually you die slowly and incredibly painfully.'

Hintu continued. 'To get the venom they milk the snake and put it onto a dart. Then the convicted person is taken deep into the rainforest blindfolded and released to make a run for it. The men of the village hunt you down, treating you like their prey, and attempt to hit you with the poisonous dart. If you're lucky, you die quickly if you're not...' he trailed off.

The three fell silent and reflected on their destiny.

'When will this happen?' Megan didn't really want to hear the answer but had asked it anyway.

'Tomorrow morning – once judgement has been made they don't delay.'

*

With their words still ringing in her head, Megan struggled to sleep. In fact sleep was not forthcoming at all. Instead she watched the other two doze off.

As she thought about the council meeting the night before, anger filled every corner of her mind. Millions of thoughts raced randomly through her brain. She wondered if the legal system in her own country was any better. Did injustice just flow from every decision? She thought about what she would have done with her life had she been allowed to reach adulthood. Now she would never know.

She also thought about her parents for the first time since she arrived. Would they miss her? Probably not, she decided. But she hadn't missed them either. Everyone she had loved was now gone.

Out of curiosity, she looked out of the window to see how they were locked in. A wooden bar was slid across the door with a padlock holding it fast. She stared intently at it. The bar started to tremor and shake and shudder until it burst off. In the silence, the shattered padlock echoed around the village as it clattered to the floor. Megan waited to see if anyone stirred. No one did.

'Cayru, Hintu, wake up,' Megan whispered urgently. 'We've got to go.'

Slipping noiselessly and unseen out of the hut, the children vanished into the rainforest.

'How are we going to prove our innocence?' Cayru questioned once they'd found a safe place to temporarily rest.

'I've no idea,' Hintu answered. And he really didn't.

'Then what are we going to do?' Cayru persisted.

'Hope for a lot of luck,' chimed in Megan, who was starting to feel like this madness was happening to someone else.

Megan couldn't quite put her finger on it but she felt like they were being watched; being protected. Every time she glanced behind, the figure just evaporated. All that was left was a haze like heat rising from the ground.

'I'm sure I'm going mad. If I haven't already,' Megan muttered to herself.

Chapter 12

Justice Must Be Done

The early morning mist hung just above the surface of the river as a faint hum of a motorboat was heard making its way down the river. At the helm was the solution to the tribal leader's problem. The boat emerged from the mist and moored alongside the village's riverbank. Only one villager was there to see his arrival – Latifah, and she had been waiting for him.

'Kenji, you came, you got my message.'

'Yes, Mother. I was always close by to watch over you. And of course I always know your call.' Kenji hugged his mother, both relieved and apprehensive about returning home. They had a deep spiritual connection: you could say a magical one.

'Where are the others?' Latifah asked looking past Kenji to see if they were in the boat.

Hunched at the bow of the boat was a bundle of orange fur. They stirred when they heard her voice. Latifah gently picked them up to carry them to the village. They were still very thin and weak but were starting to gain strength.

It was a heart-warming sight to watch these silent figures emerge from the foliage and enter the confines of the village. Saran, the tribal leader and Latifah's husband, was the first to bear witness to this vision. However, he was not so pleased to see this sight; his face was like thunder seeing his younger son return to the village. He'd been banished, the laws clearly stated that his banishment was for life, breaking that law meant certain death. Saran then looked at his wife, who stood resolute and defiant.

'You must listen to your younger son.'

Saran turned his back on them to walk away.

'Where is your wisdom that you were once known and revered for? When you were a young man you had the skill and compassion to listen to your people, the stars, our ancestors, the forest and the animals that we share our home with. Has your heart hardened so much that you cannot see or feel love any more? Can you not hear pain or know justice? I never ask you to do anything as I trust you to do what is right but this time you are blinded and you have been deceived. At least listen and then make your decision. There are many sides to a story – all are the truth.'

Saran stopped in his tracks. He knew there and then that life was never going to be the same. That although tradition was good so too was change.

'Come this way. Latifah make us tea and I can talk with my son. We must also feed the orang-utans, they look half-starved.' Saran had softened slightly and knew that his wife, as usual, was talking common sense.

In the security of the tribal leader's hut, Kenji narrated the events of the past couple of days. Nayla waited till Kenji had finished before she told her story. Saran was relieved but hugely saddened at hearing his older son's actions.

'We must talk to the children,' Saran proposed. 'Can you bring them here?'

Latifah shuffled her feet awkwardly and hesitated momentarily before she confessed that the children were no longer in the village.

Unfortunately, Faisa had already discovered this and had organised for the hunters to load up their darts and start the hunt. After all, they had been tried and convicted. Justice must be done.

Chapter 13

The Snake in the Grass

All three children needed to rest but were nervous about staying in the same place for too long.

'Oooww!' yelped Hintu.

'What?' Cayru exclaimed.

Hintu reached down and grasped his ankle. 'I've been bitten.'

Cayru quickly searched the undergrowth to find the biting critter. To her horror she could see the brown and chalk-white, angular face of the Malayan Pit Viper – a snake that was not scared of humans. Normally a snake would slither off but not this one, it stood its ground which meant they were not safe.

'We have to get away from here!' the desperation in Cayru's voice was evident.

Hintu couldn't stand so the girls picked him up. It's amazing where you find the strength when danger is so close and Cayru and Megan certainly managed to find it now.

Beads of sweat rolled off his forehead and he was starting to mumble. A fever was taking over.

Placing him down, the girls noticed that his ankle had swollen to twice its size with blisters popping up all around the bitten area. Hintu was struggling to breathe, his breath was getting shorter and shallower. They could hear him rasping.

'What do we need to do?' Megan asked.

'I've no idea but I do know that if this isn't dealt with soon he'll definitely die.'

Megan sensed rather than saw the shimmer; looking across to where she thought it was, the shimmer transformed into a figure. Once fully formed, the figure moved into the light.

'Latifah!' Megan gulped.

'Ssshhh, child. Cayru can't see me. I'll give you the

instructions on how to heal Hintu. It means you have to be brave and venture off the path to collect the right plants.' Latifah went on to explain which plants she would need and what to do. 'I must go now, I have other work to do,' and with that she vanished.

To Cayru's surprise, Megan shot off without a word only to return fifteen minutes later with a collection of plants. She carefully followed the instructions and waited to see what would happen. To her relief Hintu's breathing started to return to normal.

'How did you know what to do?' Cayru asked a little perplexed.

'A little luck and a lot of magic,' she answered glibly.

Before they had time to congratulate themselves, they could hear the heavy tramping of the huntsmen through the rainforest. The village men were shouting to each other. The hunt was on.

Chapter 14

Ancestral Guidance

'We need to get out of here and fast,' Megan whispered stating the obvious.

The two girls picked Hintu up, one on each arm and dragged him through the dense forest avoiding the paths.

'Which way?'

Megan looked around and saw the now familiar shimmer. 'This way.'

They continued to follow the shimmer of light until they came back to the village. Not somewhere they had expected but Megan had to trust the shimmer. With the men out looking for them, the village was deserted except for the smiling face of Latifah.

'Quick, this way,' she urgently indicated to them to hide in the hut that stood just outside the sight of the village. She already had the forest medicine for Hintu laid out on the table.

'How… how… did you know?' spluttered Cayru.

Megan and Latifah just glanced knowingly at each other.

'Nayla!' Megan couldn't believe who she was seeing. She ran over and hugged Nayla and Lomon. Lomon looked deep in to Megan's eyes and leant across to hug her. He pouted his lips and gave Megan a wet sloppy kiss on her cheek. Megan giggled with joy at seeing her old friends knowing that they were safe.

What she hadn't seen was a little ginger shape lying motionless in the corner but Cayru had.

Cayru moved slowly over to the inert figure, scared at what she might find.

'Iago?' With the sound of Cayru's gentle voice, Iago jumped up and scurried round the room yipping and yelping, jumping on the furniture and knocking cups and bottles over. She eventually jumped up into

Cayru's arms and proceeded to prod and pull her face, showering her with orang-utan kisses.

'I think she's pleased to see you,' Latifah laughed.

When Saran entered the room, both Cayru and Megan jumped back into the shadows. They were terrified at his presence. It was then that they saw Kenji sitting quietly in the corner. Cayru couldn't believe that he'd come back.

'Megan, this is Kenji, he's Faisa's brother. He'd been banished many years ago. He helped me escape from Faisa.' She turned to Kenji. 'How did you get Iago back?'

'I followed the men and waited for them to drink themselves to sleep. It wasn't difficult they were pretty stupid.'

The distant sound of angry men could be heard approaching the village. It was very evident that the huntsmen were not happy and completely confused how their prey had slipped past them somehow. The tribal leader waited for them to return. Once they had all arrived back, Saran ordered them to take their seat in the circle. They knew by the sound of his voice that something was not right.

He waited until silence descended and that all the men had realised the seriousness of the situation. There was an audible gasp when Kenji emerged from the hut. Faisa was about to protest but with just a look from Saran, he stopped in his tracks and decided this was not the time to object.

'We have two decisions to make, men of the Manyak village. First, my honoured family, I want to invite Nayla and Iago into the circle.' There was a murmur from the men as this was unusual to call upon an animal to give evidence. It went against all the ancestral laws.

'Silence,' roared Saran.

Both Nayla and Iago had been clinging to Kenji's legs. He gently led them to the centre of the circle and from there they told their story. Nayla told how

Megan had saved hers and Lomon's life until Megan was caught by Faisa. Iago then followed telling them how she was caught and sold by Faisa. The evidence was stacking up against him; he had no smart answer now.

'I think we can safely say that the children are innocent and that their sentence to death has to be renounced. Do you agree?'

Without any hesitation, each and every one placed their voting stick into the circle. Justice had been done. But what about Faisa?

'I said we had two decisions. Our second decision is to decide what should happen to Faisa; he has cheated, lied, stolen, kidnapped, bullied and hurt many people along the way. He falsely accused the children of his own crime and, by the Manyak law, that means death.'

'NO!' Kenji interjected. 'We've had enough of death, there's too much of it, we need to change our laws. I cannot stand by and watch my brother die.' Kenji turned to Faisa and said, 'You have constantly dishonoured this tribe, what punishment do you think should be yours?'

This was new. No one had ever been asked that before.

Faisa hung his head in shame and thought for a moment before replying. 'I shall leave the village until I can bring honour and earn your trust again. I will learn how to protect our forest, our home, our ways.'

He stood up and left the village with nothing, not even a goodbye.

'My young son, you have been fair and just and for that I make you the next tribal leader. Are we agreed?'

With the whooping and hollering, the men demonstrated that they were very happy with the suggestion.

'We must celebrate.' From then on the villagers, Megan and the orang-utans, danced, ate and drank till the light glimmered just above the horizon. There was one person, however, who didn't celebrate and he slipped away into the night. Only one person saw him go, and that was his wife.

Latifah knew that her husband had gone to join his ancestors. She had watched him over the last couple of months in great pain even though he'd tried to hide it from her. His body was weary and his work was done. Latifah knew that she would see him again but not in this life.

His body was found the next day and buried with great ceremony as was befitting a great leader.

Chapter 15

Home is Where the Heart is Not

'Cayru, Hintu, you need to go back to the village – you have your duties to finish.' Sugito beckoned.

Reluctantly, they left Megan alone with the orang-utans to continue playing.

Checking behind her to see if she was alone, Megan attached some fruit to a branch and, with her new-found magical ability, teased Iago and Lomon by dangling it just in front of them. The branch would dance and the orang-utans would follow. To encourage and teach them to climb trees, Megan floated the branch up the trees watching the mad creatures fighting and scrambling over the top of each other to reach the ripe mangoes.

When they were bored with that, she would play her piccolo and delight in them dancing in circles around each other in time to the music. She would also hover sticks over their heads and drop them on other unsuspecting orang-utans where they would look up into the trees, spot an innocent orang-utan and blame them.

Amongst the smaller orang-utans, a scrap would break out. Megan had never seen so many temper tantrums or sulks; they were just like human children. Despite their sulks and tantrums, they were incredibly affectionate to a point it became highly demanding. Iago and Lomon were great friends but would get very jealous if one was having a cuddle with Megan.

Megan loved this new life but knew at some point she would have to return to her old one. Very quickly she would push the thought to the back of her mind. Her life here was loving and fun but back home it was cold and friendless.

As she was moving things around to tease the baby orang-utans, Latifah appeared from the shadows. Megan quickly dropped all the objects hoping she hadn't been seen.

'My dear, you really mustn't use your powers here, if you were spotted…' Latifah trailed off, reluctant to talk about death or harsh punishments. She too had many magical powers and all her life she'd had to hide it. She was tired of that. And any way that wasn't what she wanted to talk to Megan about.

At that moment they heard the whistling of the Hard Rock Café T-shirt man coming round the corner, his wheelbarrow laden with fruits for the mischievous and hungry orang-utans.

'It's time for you to leave us.'

'No, I really don't want to go, Latifah. I'm happy here,' protested Megan.

'But, my child, this is not your destiny. We have become your family and we care and love you deeply but you have another family.'

Latifah was only speaking out loud Megan's inner thoughts.

Looking down at her piccolo, Megan remembered where the whole journey had begun.

Latifah continued, handing over an ornamental jade axe, 'Thaddeus left this behind for you and asked me to give you it when I thought it was time for you to return. You've been with us for many weeks now and we have enjoyed your company but you must go back to the life you own. You have taught us many things and helped us bring great change. We thank you for that but you know you have to leave us. Take this *kapak jed nenek moyang*[1], it will guide you back to your own time and land.'

Megan took the axe and stared at it trying really hard not to cry. She listened intently to Latifah and knew that she was right.

---

1   Ancestral jade axe

'But will I…' when Megan looked up she realised that Latifah had gone.

No goodbyes, no wise final words, she just vanished.

Megan burned the image of the orang-utans one last time into her memory, they had become her family and she had to leave them now not knowing whether they would ever meet again. Or whether they would be safe.

'Okay, my *kapak jed nenek moyang*, tell me what to do.' At first there was no response. Then a distant voice could be heard. The more she listened the closer it came till it was swirling around her head. She listened harder until the words became louder and clearer.

Megan raised the axe and sliced the air in front of her. To her surprise there seemed to be a tear in the fabric of time and space. She peered inside and saw the familiar dusty bookshop. She stepped through the tear with huge sadness and immense regret, back to a time and place she hated. Before she could change her mind the opening disappeared. There was no going back.

'Home seems to be where the heart is not,' Megan spoke out loud.

'You're back then.' She spun round to see Thaddeus. His face showed that he understood Megan's sadness. She silently handed back the axe and allowed the tears to roll freely down her cheek.

He placed his hand on her shoulder. 'You must be careful with that book it could take you anywhere or to any time in history or to the future. You were lucky this time but it can be very dangerous stepping into a time or place that you know very little about.'

Megan nodded imperceptibly and promised that she wouldn't open the book again.

Chapter 16

The Island of Borneo

Megan stood staring at the front of her house, a house she hadn't even slept in. It wasn't her home really, the Manyaks were her home. She took a deep breath and entered the cold empty hallway. She had changed but her real world hadn't.

'Ah Megan, there you are. Go upstairs and get changed we have visitors coming over for dinner soon,' her mother rushed past her not even giving her a second glance.

'Welcome home, Megan, did you have a nice time, Megan?' Megan said sarcastically to herself.

Up in her room she lay on her bed thinking about the friends she had gained and lost and the kindness she'd been shown. Now her life was as cold and as empty as the hallway.

148

School tomorrow – another thing she dreaded.

Leaning over to turn the television on, she was horrified to watch a report on the blazing fires racing through the Indonesian rainforests on the island of Borneo.

'Wasn't that where I was?' Megan exclaimed. 'It must be as that is the only place orang-utans live in the wild.'

She couldn't believe that more land was being decimated.

They panned across so Megan could see thousands of acres being deliberately destroyed and thousands more destined to go the same way.

'*For the sake of palm oil, many thousands of indigenous tribes have lost their homes and hundreds of orang-utans have been killed or displaced. If this forest destruction continues, then these beloved orang-utans will have vanished from the wild within the next five to ten years if nothing is done,*' the news reporter related solemnly. '*The global demand for palm oil has attracted producers to clear more land. More land equals more palm oil, which in turn, equals more money. There is little or no consideration for the rainforest and the endangered species that live there. Soon the tiger, rhino, orang-utan and sun bear will become extinct from the shores of Borneo. Once gone never to be seen again. Already the Javan tiger, which was indigenous to the island of Java – one of the Indonesian islands – is extinct. Humans are merciless with their takeover of the planet. We must remember that we share this planet; we don't own it.'*

Megan sat shocked and unable to think clearly. There was a chance that the Manyak tribe and their orang-utan friends had lost everything. Megan had no way of finding out if they were safe. Once again she felt helpless, alone and miserable.

Still wracked with guilt and unhappiness, Megan found her way to her new school. On her first day, the teacher asked each pupil to present a topic to the class. It could be on anything. Megan suddenly sat upright very interested, knowing exactly what she would talk about. A little glimmer of hope started to shine. A way forward at last.

Chapter 17

The Presentation

It was the day of the presentation. Megan had worked hard researching and practising but was still incredibly nervous.

Clutching her notes, she watched the other presentations: Tommy talked about his favourite football team; Ali rambled on explaining how to make your own computer and Priya's passion was cooking. All of them had talked for far too long.

Megan watched the class as they yawned their way through each presentation. Miss Yeoman had to keep reminding them how important it was to respect other people's presentations by sitting still and listening properly. After each one, the class were asked if they wanted to ask a question or make a positive comment.

There were a few questions by the boys after Tommy's, but they were boring. Nobody had anything good to say except they liked football.

A few pupils fell asleep during Ali's as it was very long and complicated. No one knew what to ask because they hadn't understood it. The only comment made was that Ali must be very clever.

Priya explained how to make a cake. Megan knew her presentation was next so had stopped listening by then.

'This is boring, Miss!' shouted Danny. He found everything boring but in this instance Megan agreed with him.

'Danny, if you think this is boring then when you do your presentation make sure you make it interesting and fun,' Miss Yeoman suggested.

'Do we really have to listen to another one, Miss?' asked Simran. 'I'm going to die of boredom.'

'Yes,' chanted the class. 'Please, Miss!'

'Absolutely not. We have Megan's presentation and then you can go out and play.' This comment prompted the boys to pester Miss Yeoman for play now, not after the next talk. All they had in their heads was a game of football, not another tedious talk on something they really weren't interested in.

'It's okay, Miss, I'm happy to do it another time,' Megan offered.

The class all agreed with Megan but Miss Yeoman insisted that the presentations continue.

Megan was dreading it. She was close to bolting from the classroom but knew that this was a chance to tell her story. Or rather the orang-utan's story.

'Megan, please come up and get yourself organised.'

The class were getting restless behind her. It was made worse by the fact that she had a technical failure. Eventually, Ali came to her rescue, after all he was a computer whizz. Megan was relieved and felt a bit guilty that she had had such negative feelings about him earlier.

It took Miss Yeoman five minutes to settle the class down.

'If you don't behave, then I will keep you in over break,' she reprimanded.

By now Megan was falling apart inside. Her palms started to sweat and her voice became squeaky and shaky.

'Oh no this is going to be worse than the others,' Danny interrupted.

'What's your talk about, Megan?' Miss Yeoman ignored him and focused on Megan.

'Orang-utans,' she answered.

This was the signal to set the whole class off. Up they jumped racing round the class imitating orang-utans.

Megan's feelings very quickly changed from nervousness to anger.

'Sit down!' she barked. 'Show some respect.'

The children stopped and looked at her, surprised by her outcry.

'I'll take up ten minutes of your time, if you don't like it I'll stop. Okay?'

'Fair enough,' they agreed.

*

'Who looks after the orang-utans?' Megan announced.

She then went on to tell them the story of Iola and Iago, and how Iola was killed and Iago was kidnapped. She told them about the rescue of Iago, Nayla and Lomon, describing the devastation of the rainforest for palm oil plantations. The children were transfixed. As promised, after ten minutes, she paused to ask them if they wanted to stop.

'Absolutely not!' exclaimed Danny.

So Megan continued. No one spoke, no one fell asleep or yawned and no one fidgeted. They had lost themselves in the story. She went on…

Old Man of the Forest.

*Who is the old man of the forest? These are the orang-utans. (*Megan showed the class a short video clip of some baby orang-utans chasing each other and then fighting with a cardboard box.*) They are only found in the wild on the islands of Sumatra and Borneo.*

Borneo is the third largest island in the world; it is found north-west of Australia. The island is divided up into three parts: Malaysia, Indonesia and Brunei. Since 2007, over half the land area of Borneo has been deforested. With this loss orang-utans, pygmy elephants, pygmy rhinoceros and sun bears, to name a few, have all lost their home.

Unfortunately, man is rapidly removing their habitat to make way for regimented plantations of palm oil trees. As a result they have been categorised as critically endangered. In the next five years there will be no wild orang-utans left.

They are supposed to be protected but companies, who are clearing the land, pay loggers and farmers money to just kill and bury the bodies otherwise the land clearing would have to cease and companies would lose money. Companies really don't want the government to intervene.

These companies are clearing land to make way for the plantation of palm oil trees. This is a cheap oil that large companies use in biscuits, bread, chocolate, skin care, detergents, make-up and shampoo. The list is endless because over half the products found in super-markets contain palm oil. And the demand for palm oil is increasing. The European Union is the third largest consumer after India and Indonesia.

The orang-utan is not the only animal affected by deforestation for palm oil. In other countries buffalo, chimpanzees, gorillas and manatees are also victims of this thirst for palm oil.

Deforestation is also due to fires, which are deliberately lit every year to quickly clear the land. Unfortunately, as a consequence, other areas of the rainforest are acci-dentally set alight by the fire's embers that float on the wind travelling great distances. This makes the fires more widespread and destructive. Sadly, last year over 100,000 people died from the smoke fumes. The number of animals killed has not been recorded but I bet there have been many hundreds of thousands.

Orang-utans are also being killed by illegal hunters for food, money or fear. They are an easy target because they are large and move slowly. The females are particularly vulnerable when they have an offspring. The mother is killed and the orphaned baby is taken either as a pet or to be sold to zoos or private collectors. Over 500 orang-utans were stolen and sold last year for hundreds of pounds each. Some people even paid up to £50 for just the skull of an orang-utan. When there is a market for live and dead orang-utans, then people will poach and sell them.

'What do we need to do?' asked Simran.

'Yeah how can we help?' Danny questioned eagerly.

There are several ways. Pass on the information through social media, this way we can educate people. Secondly, I can give you a list of products that are good and others that are really bad to buy. Ask your parents to only buy palm oil free products or products that use sustainable palm oil. And finally, you could donate money to the charities such as the Borneo Orangutan Survival Foundation so they can look after orphaned orang-utans, heal sick ones and purchase land to release them back into the wild.

When Megan had finished, the class remained silent. They were moved by her story.

'That was brilliant, Miss,' Danny was unusually enthusiastic.

'I think you need to tell, Megan, Danny.'

'That was really sad but brilliant,' he repeated.

After a few quiet moments, the class erupted into a spontaneous applause.

Many of her classmates were keen to ask her lots of questions and hear more about her adventure. Megan answered them all confidently and passionately. When the bell rang for break, no one wanted to go out – they all wanted to talk more about Borneo and the orang-utans.

'OK, class, when you get back we will talk more about how we can help.'

The class left noisily, all chatting about the story and sharing their ideas on how they could make a difference.

Megan knew that it was her mission to tell the orang-utans' story and fight their corner. She had never felt so useful; it gave her a purpose in life. Having a purpose gave her a strength that she had never felt before.

She decided to give up feeling a victim and start taking control of her life. There are people and animals struggling to stay alive and have to fight injustice every day.

She realised that it is important to live in harmony with planet earth and not destroy its beauty for greed and profit. These were the thoughts going through her head on her way home. It had been a good day at school – a really good day.

Further Information

To find out more information on palm oil and help you buy either palm oil free products or products that use sustainable palm oil go to

1. Ethical Consumer - http://www.ethicalconsumer. org/shoppingethically/palmoilfreelist.aspx
2. World Wild Life - https://www.worldwildlife.org/ pages/which-everyday-products-contain-palm-oil
3. Rainforest Foundation UK - http://www.rain-forestfoundationuk.org/palmoil - this website has a link to a document which shows you how to be a responsible shopper. This list is not definitive. There are many other products that have not been included that do not contain any palm oil.

4. Shop Palm Oil Free - https://www.shoppalmoilfree.co.uk
5. Act for Wildlife - https://www.actforwildlife.org.uk/get-involved/take-conservation-action/take-the-sustainable-palm-oil-challenge/shopping-list/

Considering over 50% of our products contain palm oil, it can be very difficult to buy palm oil free goods. However, there are organisations which monitor whether it is sustainable. Look out for the RSPO or Green Palm labels; these indicate that palm oil was produced in a socially and environmentally responsible way.